CADAVERS

A Novella
Ash Ericmore

Written by: Ash Ericmore

Copyright © 2020 Ash Ericmore

All Rights Reserved. This is a work of fiction. No part of this publication may be reproduced, distributed, or transmitted in any form or by any means, except in the case of brief quotations embodied in critical reviews.

ISBN: 9798353987710

"It is within the category of the destructive madmen that one needs to situate certain patients to whom I would like to give the name of necrophiliacs."

~ Physician Joseph Guislain 1850

Part 1
~
WES

CHAPTER 1

"Sod it." Wes pushed the shovel into the dirt, letting out a little chuckle. Sod. Jesus Christ. This never got any easier. Not ever. He pushed the shovel down. Tipped it back with the handle. And then stooped, hefted. And up. Sling. The dirt out the hole. Into the pile.

Sounded easy, right?

Yeah, well it was. The first hundred times. The thing was—he shovelled another load out—was that everyone thought that was easy. Digging holes. That big. That's why they don't use grave diggers anymore. They use machines. Big fuck off machines. Long gone were the days. Well, at least around there. There were dim shadows in the graveyard. The trees were hanging out, blocking the light of the night sky. See, in a film, something like that, exhuming a grave would take a matter of minutes. You'd see the plucky hero push the shovel in. Ten minutes later, and a five foot hole, the shovel would bang on the wood of the coffin. It wasn't actually like that. It took consummate planning for a start.

Mostly because of how long the fucking thing took.

See, having done this a few times now—and started going down the gym, not only to look good for the ladies, but also to be able to do *this*—Wes found he could get to the body in about four hours. It did depend on the wetness of the soil, of course. If it had been raining on and off for a few days, which it did frequently due to the British weather, then the dig was far easier. He could knock ten to fifteen percent off the work time. If it was dry as a bone—or August, as he knew it—then he could spend a further hour sometimes. Sure, the soil was always a bit wet, loose, the further he went down, but it was that top soil. The first couple of feet.

Of course, that didn't account for the first one. The first one he dug up had been in the ground a couple of years. He liked to think of it more as a trial run, than an absolute fucking disaster. But that one was solid fucking packed earth, all the way down. *And* an utter waste of time.

Anyway.

Timing. That was what it came down to. You see digging a grave is a long, laborious process. Four to five hours. And it wasn't like you could stop half way, and take the rest of the day off. One and done. Dig it up and fill it in. One night. But it wasn't dusk until dawn either. You had to do the whole job in the darkness. Another reason not to try to complete the task in June. The longest days. Which would suggest December, as it had shorter days. Longer nights. Around those parts, it wasn't too bad. Most of the weather around Christmas was pissy, so that helped. Not like February when the ground was frozen. Anyway.

He needed to start the job after the graveyard was clear of folks.

Now most folks, they tend not to come to graveyards after dark. It's weird. Creepy. You dig? But there are other people that will. Some kids like to go down there at night and just drink. It's quiet. They can do what they want. They can fuck around and no one cares. Drinking in public isn't legal, but you ain't gonna find a hobby bobby down there in the middle of the night.

So there's that to consider.

Then there's the weirdos. The occasional couple who want to fuck on a grave. He had never understood that. He was actually there. One time. Digging away. Heard someone coming. Put pay to him actually doing shit all from that point on. He just had to wait in his hole and hope that no one came looking. A few minutes later they were banging away like it was their honeymoon. Maybe it was? Either way, they were only there a few minutes, and then they were off. Quick on the draw, apparently. Still. She seemed satisfied.

Judging by the noise, anyway.

So he found that Friday nights and Saturday nights were off limits in the inner town graveyards. They were the sort of places that kids drank in, and usually on *those* days. So he headed to the out of town graveyard. It was only a couple of miles out, but far enough that he shouldn't see any kids. Wes had always preferred to work at the weekend too. He did have to work on Mondays.

But that was where he nearly got caught by the two fucking. He guessed they thought the same as him, and there wouldn't be anyone at a graveyard that you had to hike to or drive to. Not in the middle of the night.

So Wes found himself at a graveyard in the middle of fucking nowhere. Couple of miles outside a small village half an hour south of London. Didn't even know what the place was called. Just found it on a map. Tried his luck. Used a torch and found someone who had been down in the dirt for a couple of months. Maybe three.

Shouldn't be a problem. He started digging at ten. Seemed quiet enough. Should be finished in plenty of time. Have the hole refilled by five. Be on his way.

Wes pushed the shovel into the dirt and there was a clonk.

Hit wood.

CHAPTER 2

The secret was not to make it look like he'd been there. Honestly. That was just it, really. If no one knew, then no one would come looking. That was why he needed the time to refill the hole and such. In the films they just left the hole open. Like on Supernatural. It's no wonder the police were all up in *their* shit.

They left too much evidence. Too many questions.

He was scraping the dirt off the top of the coffin. Wes didn't want to try and get the lid open when there was dirt all over it. Been there. Done that. Mess everywhere. Utterly useless. He looked at the cut of the wood. It was a cheaper looking box. That wasn't always a bad thing. Hard to tell from the stones. In years past, the richer families had massive statues erected to celebrate the dead. Not so much these days. Without researching, Wes wouldn't know what he might find. That was fine. He didn't really want the rich. Just in case someone did make that you've dug up their sister. Or mum. Some shit.

According to the stone, this one was a loving wife and mother. Only twenty five.

That was the other problem.

It would be best to know how they died. You know. Before all the effort. If they'd been in some horrible motoring accident, they could be in all sorts of a mess. Nobody wants that, do they? Still. You pays your money and you takes your chance. As they say.

Not that there's any money changing hands.

Wes had brought a crowbar with him. First time, he tried to crowbar the thing open without undoing the latches. Good times. He knew better than that now. All a learning curve. Undo the latches on the coffin. Even the cheap ones have rudimentary latches. The crowbar is in case the wood has swollen. Happens under the soil. That, or the gasses from the body have released. That can warp the wood too. If that was the case, Wes would likely just close it back up and fill in the hole. He poked around in a corpse once that had gone to the point of combustion.

What a mess.

Wes could tell now. Pull up the lid and the smell. That was the first thing. As Wes understood, they smelt for a while—a few days—then the smell goes away. Comes back a few weeks later, for a few months, when the body starts to really breakdown. He was looking for one in the sweet spot. Not smelling anymore from death. Not smelling because it hadn't started to decompose.

Sweet.

Anyway. Got the dirt off. Undo the latches. Might need the crowbar. Might not. Hopefully she'll be in the sweet spot. Not been in a car accident. It was the excitement that got to Wes at that point. On his knees. Readying himself. Always the same.

He'd scratched away enough soil from down the side of the coffin to get his feet down there. Stand with one leg each side of it, to open it. He didn't do that once. Tried for fifteen minutes to open the fucking lid.

Standing on it.

What a twat. Never drink and exhume. Never. Also makes the actual digging part harder. Once, his mum had a bunch of Irish guys around to dig her a new driveway—not a euphemism—and those fuckers drank Guinness all day. *All day*. Probably could have gotten the job done faster if they'd been sober.

Anyway. Wes got his feet down the side of the coffin.

This is it. Love at first sight? Ready to meet the missus?

His fingers were shaking slightly. Could be the exertion. Could be the excitement. Deep breath in. One to help take the edge off the nerves. One to hold in, just in case she stinks like a joint of meat that's been left out overnight in the middle of summer.

Pop the lid.

There's a hiss. Gas escaping. That's a good sign. Means the box was sealed correctly. No … bugs. No smell either. He pushed the lid back. Opening it like a shoe box. Lean the lid against the soil. The side of the hole. Look at his prize. She's … beautiful. That much is undeniable. Her cheeks have caved in slightly. That's her age. Getting older, does that to you. Lack of moisture. He can fix that. He can make her moist.

That came out wrong.

Or did it?

Focus. Looking down her body, he guessed that it wasn't a car accident. That was good. No smell. Might have a winner here. Wes stood, straight. His head out of the hole. Looked around the graveyard. Nothing. Not so much as a sound. Perfect.

There's a cool mist though. Probably the height of the place. The graveyard is on high ground. He leant back down. Rested his hand on hers. It was laying over her chest. Her flesh was cold. He should get her inside. Back to his. Somewhere it was warm. Somewhere, they can get to know each other. "Oh," he said. "My names Wesley. Wes. You can call me Wes." He glanced back up to the stone. Towering above him. Leanne Balls.

Balls.

Stupid name.

"Leanne," she said. "Hello, Wes."

He looked back down at her. She wasn't speaking really. He just liked to hear the voices in his head. It made them more real. Made the relationship more real. The love.

Besides. He liked to hear them calling his name.

Wes leant down. Took her hands. People always assume that rigor mortis sets in and stayed. It doesn't. Rigor only lasts a few days. Then the bodies go … floppy … again. Just as well. No one wants to be with someone who's frigid, do they?

Wes pulled her up. Got her close to standing. The shape of the coffin helped with that. Kept her legs rigid. He would have loved to spend more time getting to know her there, but he knew he didn't have that luxury. Time was of the essence, remember? Once she was close to standing, they embraced. He could manoeuvre her around and use his knee to boost her up, sitting her on the edge of the grave. Then push her backwards so she's out.

Then Wes climbed out. Went and unlocked the car.

Always keep the car locked. You never know what ragamuffins might be out there.

He would have preferred to put her in the boot. If someone saw them together, they might not understand. But he didn't. He carried her over to the car, slipped her in the front seat. She was light. It's the mild decomposition that has occurred. Should be fine. As he leant over her and pulled the seat belt across, he got a whiff of something unsavoury. Hm. Hopefully she hasn't gone too far. Better check the dates on the headstone. Make sure she's not past her best before.

Wes slammed the door.

Locked the car.

Back to the hole. He climbed down back into the grave. Pulled the lid down and closed the coffin. It's amazing how many tricks you learnt on the job. First time he pulled out a body, he just started filling in the hole. Didn't think about it. When he'd finished, there wasn't enough soil. With the coffin open, he was a good eight inches of soil short to re-fill the whole hole. Had to start stealing shovels full of it from other places. A right mess. Couldn't believe he got away with it.

With the coffin closed, he pushed himself back up, out of the hole. Got the crowbar, and took it to the car. Chucked it in the boot. The last thing he needed was to leave some evidence behind. Back to the coffin. Started pushing the dirt back in. He'd tried to speed this process up several times but hadn't found a good way of doing it. There didn't seem to be a short cut. So, using the shovel like a broom at first, he swept the dirt back in. Once there was little of it left, he scooped the dirt with his hands. It seemed the most efficient way. Still thought there had to be a better way. Pad the dirt down.

And then there was the secret.

When Wes first started. Before he went all hefting dirt about. He rolled the top layer off. Like he was rolling turf. If he didn't, when he had finished, it looked like a freshly dug grave.

Then, he put the rolls of sod and turf down and unrolled them. In a couple of days, even the groundskeeper wouldn't be able to tell.

And he hadn't been caught. So it must work.

He took the torch. Shovel. Anything else. Back to the car, in the boot. Wes brought a container of water with him. Washed his hands. Just rudimentarily. He could do it all properly later. Took a drink of some of it. It's good to hydrate.

CHAPTER 3

Clean getaway. So to speak. Wes always felt better once he was moving. It was usually around four or five when he got back to the house. There weren't a lot of people on the road at that time. There was certainly no police presence.

Safe enough, he thought. He chanced a glance at Leanne. She had her eyes shut. Looked asleep. As it should be. That time of the morning. He looked at the clock on the dash. Fucking hell. The sun would be up soon. Better get her home. He put his foot down harder on the accelerator. He used to live in the town. No way this sort of shit would fly there.

No way.

His old man popped his clogs a few years back. Left him the house. It was an old property. Needed some work to get it ready for company. But that was fine. Something to keep him busy on the cold nights alone.

The house was on a patch of land just outside a small village. Off the coast, still in Kent. His old stomping ground. Back when he was a little shitbag. Knocking on peoples doors and running away. Scrumping apples. Showing his cock to the girls behind the bike shed. For money. Of course. He got nothing else out of it, after all.

Back then he enjoyed the little things that more … country living … gave. Once, his mum caught him with a dead squirrel. He was keeping it under the bed. Snuck food off his plate for it. She didn't understand, of course. His old man said he wasn't right in the head. But he loved that thing.

Ended up seeing a doctor for about three years after that. They kept making him go until he lied, and said that what he'd done was wrong and that the squirrel shouldn't have ever been picked up. It's not like he fucked it or anything. Well … that one time, but that didn't count.

After that, he learned that he needed to keep his secrets to himself. The parents didn't understand. Then, later, he found that society really didn't either.

He pulled the car off the road through the gates and onto his driveway.

There were parts of society that claimed to understand, but he could only seem to touch base with them on the internet, and they all seemed a little … weird. He didn't want to be rude, of course, but they didn't seem to have any limits or boundaries. Seemed to think that watching people have sex with one thing was the same as having sex with another. Which it wasn't. He'd witnessed some messed up shit that would turn anyone's hair white.

He looked over to Leanne. Blew her a little kiss. She was still sleeping.

Stopped the car outside the front door. The sun was going to rise soon. Only minutes away. He'd made it. He always made it. But time was short. There was a small distance between the house and the road, but there were no street lights on that road. Meant that during the night hours he was alone there. Once the sun was up, anyone on the street could see the front door. He jumped out and hurried around to Leanne's side of the car and opened the door. He stroked her cheek, gently with the back of his hand. She was cool.

Over to the front door. He opened it up. Left it wide. Back to the car. He looked down at himself. He really was a state after all the digging. Better be sure to wash up as soon as he could. Wes leant across her and undid the belt. Slipped his hand into the divot behind Leanne's knees. Then the other behind her back. Lifted her out the car. She really was light. Which was good. Sometimes it was hard to get them out the car. Especially after all the digging.

He kicked the door shut. Went into the house. Carrying her across the threshold. Straight to the stairs and up. She was light as a feather. "It is your beauty that gives me the strength, my love," he whispered as he whipped her up the stairs. Along the landing. Into the bedroom. "I'm putting you in my room," he said, coyly. "I hope you don't mind."

Of course she didn't. She was dead.

He slipped her onto the bed. Took a step back and turned the lamp on, on the bedside table. Looked her down. Stunning. It was the first time he'd seen he in the proper light. She had dark hair. It was a bit of a mess now, but that was his fault. She had hard cheekbones, like Monroe. Slim. Slender. She was dressed in her fineries. A long dark blue dress. High heels. Very sexy.

He could feel his body react to having her there. On his bed. Waiting for him. But he turned away. Didn't want to cause any embarrassment. He wasn't *clean* after all. He slipped to the doorway. Glanced back. "I won't be long," he said. "Don't go anywhere."

Wes left the room, pulling the door closed to allow her to rest. She must be tired after all that … sitting in the car. Went along the hallway to the bathroom. In. Stripped off. In the shower. The water ran brown from the dirt on him. It seemed to collect on him like a fungus. Happened every time. Like the dirt of the graveyard was somehow attracted to him. As he was *them*. Wes filled a palm with shampoo and raked it into his hair with his fingers. Massaged it into his scalp. Washed it away. He was using Radox shower gel. Had bits in it. Something supposed to relax through scent or something. He didn't really know anything about any of that, but it did smell nice. She should like it.

Rubbed it into all the bits that needed it. Cock. Balls. They were super important, because of how sweaty they got. Quick rinse under the arms too. Didn't want the pits to stink. Wes turned the shower off. It was cool in the room. He didn't shower hot. Never had. It did mean that he could still look in the mirror without wiping it down. To get the steam off. He stepped out the bath. Over to the mirror. Combed his hair. Sprayed under his arms. Something from the poundshop in the nearest town. Did a job. Not the best in the world, but Leanne shouldn't mind too much.

Talc on his balls.

No idea why. Ritual.

He went out, naked into the hallway and opened what was—once—the airing cupboard. Now it was just a cupboard. Still had a habit of putting clothes in there to air. Whatever that meant. Pulled out a pair of black boxers. Slipped them on. They were tight, not because they were supposed to be sexy-tight, but because he'd put on a few pounds lately. Needed to hit the gym a little harder.

Or maybe not. He looked down at himself. The tightness of the pants enhanced his bulge. Made his not sexy-tight boxers, sexy-tight. Hm. Bargain. Maybe that was going to work out for the best. He smiled. Everything was coming up Wesley.

He pulled a shirt out. Button up. Pulled it on, but didn't do it up. That would do. Beach casual. Sort of. He wasn't any good at accessorizing, but he was sure that he'd measure up on this occasion. He looked along the hall to the bedroom door. He was tired. Lot of work achieved. And Leanne was probably sleeping still, so he had some time. Might get something to eat.

Wes went down the stairs. Quietly. Didn't want to disturb her. Into the kitchen. He opened the fridge. Like most men, he seemed surprised that the fridge fairy hadn't been while he was out and changed the contents of the fridge for the better. "Nothing in," he muttered. There was food there. Plenty of it. He'd gone shopping less than a week ago. However, like most people, he'd purchased a few meals that looked tantalizing and awesome—treat food, basically—the usual sort of things. Pies. Fried chicken. Frozen donor kebab. And on the flip side, he'd balanced that by buying a few days of healthy, nutritious meals. Salads. Tofu. Something he couldn't pronounce that was made of mushrooms pretending to be meat. All of that shit was still in the fridge.

"Nothing in," he said, again. And let the door go, closing itself.

He opened the freezer. Pulled out a pizza. It was the last one in there. Stuffed crust. He was saving it for a special occasion. But now *was* a special occasion, he thought to himself, justifying the pizza. At six in the morning. On a work day. He looked at his watch, the pizza already out the box, as he took to gnawing at the plastic film that encased the goods. He turned the oven on. One-ninety. Everything in Wes's house cooked at one-ninety. Usually for twenty-two minutes. It rarely failed him. He went to pull his phone out his pocket. Realised it was in his trousers on the bathroom floor.

He wanted to call in sick to work. Best do it early. Then they couldn't complain that they didn't have time to call in a replacement. It meant he wouldn't get paid for the day. He looked at the ceiling.

But she was worth it.

CHAPTER 4

Wes chomped on a slice of the pizza. It wasn't bad. He was standing on the bottom stair. Looking up. Wondering if she was going to be ready. If she was awake. Rested enough. He was, after all, expecting her to do little work. He was going to do all the hard work. He chuckled.

Hard.

He chewed thoughtfully on the crust, and stepped up, one stair at a time. Quietly. He was moving quickly, though. Anticipation. Felt something odd. Glanced down at himself. Pizza sauce on his bare chest. Lucky it wasn't still hot. That could have hurt. He slid his finger through it and went to stick it in his mouth. There was a chest hair lodged in the stuff. Huh. He sighed. Plucked it out and discarded it to the air. Ate the pizza sauce. Continued up the stairs. Finished the crust of the pizza.

Went and stood at the doorway to the bedroom. Knocked lightly. Only polite, really. He pushed the door open, stepped in. She was still there, on the bed, just as he had left her. A small, cheeky smile crossed his face. She was stunning. Was going to be more stunning in a few minutes. He crossed the carpet to her. Slipped his arse down on the bed. "Hi," he whispered. Dropped his tone down a bit. Tried to get a bit more *sexy* in his voice. He took her hand from the sheet. Held it. Ice cold. "Do you mind?" he asked. Eyebrows went up. "Oh, you don't normally, but as I asked so nicely … cheeky." He kissed her pale skin. Mottled with what could have been mistaken for age spots. They weren't. Couldn't have been. She was far too young. Wes turned and let his other hand fall on her ankle, protruding from the long dress. He slid it forward. Up. Pushing the dress aside. "I know," he said. "Presumptuous. But you don't mind, do you." It wasn't a question. He got to her knee. She had a fair bit of stubble up there. Should probably shave her legs. But he wasn't in the mood to wait. He wanted to consummate. His cock had already involuntarily flopped from one side of his shorts to the other.

He let his hand go further. Cool, dry, skin. Made him hard. He reached the top of her leg. Could feel the material that stopped his fingers from roaming any further. He turned and looked at her. Her makeup was faded. Probably the gases that leaked from her over the weeks. Burned off the makeup. They always used cheap makeup. He would get her something decent. Didn't know what. Didn't have a clue. Maybelline, or Avon, or some shit. Didn't really matter. "Can I look?" he asked.

Raised himself off the bed. His cock was striking a tent pole out the front of his shorts. Yurting. "I am sorry," he blustered. "But I suppose, it is your fault." He grinned at her. Quick wink. Slid both his hands up her dress.

Found her panties. They were probably more traditional knickers, but he liked the word panties, so regardless of whether they were sexy Saturday night panties, grannie pants, or Monday to Friday office wear, he was going to call them panties.

He slid them down.

Out the bottom of the dress.

Grannie panties. Oh well.

"Sexy," he said. Mustn't give the game away. He sat. Slipped his hand up her dress. Found her cold, hard, slit. Dried. Petrified. He took a deep breath in, surprised. "My," he said, swiftly removing his hand. He slipped his forefinger into his mouth.

Wetted it.

Dove his hand back under the dress. Up. Found what he was looking for. Sort of. Couldn't quite find the entrance he knew was there. He found on another occasion that if he didn't do this first, it was much harder to get the consummation correct. Not without danger of snapping it off. Poke. Prod. "What are you, sewn up?" he grinned. "Just my little jok—" He stopped. "Bingo," he said. "We have entered the tunnel ... *of love*." He slipped his finger into what he hoped was her snatch. It was kind of fifty-fifty for a couple of moments. Until he'd wriggled about a bit. Didn't want to end up in the wrong hole, now, did he?

Wes was pretty confident he was in the right place. Slid back and forth. Circle around a bit. Yup. Definitely the right hole. He pulled his finger free. Out from the dress.

Gave it a quick sniff while his head was turned away. So she couldn't see. Didn't want to make a thing of it if she smelt like week old curry. So far so good. Turned back. Stood. Slipped out of his shirt. "Why, yes. I have been working out." Let it drop to the floor. He stood, pants still on, cock protruding from the front, with his hands on his waist. Like he was a fucking superhero.

Hell. He *was* a fucking super hero.

He yanked his boxers off his waist, twanging his wang around like a flagpole in the wind. "Enough …" shit. What was her name again? "… Darling." Stepped out the boxers. Pushed the bottom of her dress up. There was a smell under there. The dress was keeping it trapped in like old farts in Tupperware. Too late now. He parted her legs. Looking down on her beauty. Small tufts of hair protruding from her mound like she'd shaven badly—probably just a side effect of the light decomposition.

He was ready. She was ready.

He slipped in between her legs. "Prophylactics? No. You don't mind, do you?" Wes scooted in low. Almost down to missionary. He could feel her cold body under his. Boney. He got that. Understood it. He probably should have tried to hydrate her before this, but he couldn't wait. *They* couldn't. He smiled at her. His face so close to hers. Dared to lean in, and get a quick kiss. On the cheek.

We could feel the tip of his cock probing her slit. He knew that the gap he'd made with his fingers wouldn't close back up. Not for hours, so he let it tease her slightly. Let it slip and slide over her clit. His pre-cum providing all the juices he needed. She needed. *They*. He slid himself forward, into her. Deep. As deep as his fingers had gotten, then deeper. Pushing her cold, hard, cunt apart. Into the cavern of love.

Wes started, back and forth. Into a rhythm. She was rocking gently under him. He got himself comfortable. She was beautiful. This wasn't going to take long. He was sure she'd understand. It was her, you see. So beautiful.

Then a new smell appeared. From where he wasn't sure.

But it was *God-fucking-awful.* His rhythm interrupted, he slowed. "Sorry," he said, picking up speed again. Didn't want her to think there was anything wrong. That smell though. What was it? All these girls and he'd never smelt anything like that before.

Fuck.

He got up onto his hands. More of a push-up position. Get himself away from her a little. See if it was not so noticeable. Hoped it would help.

Still there.

It had put him right off his stride, and his excitement to finish waned. He slowed. Slid out of her, and up, onto his knees. "I'm sorry," he said, his knees still between her legs, towering over her. He started stroking his cock. Knock one out. On her tits. Yes.

He let himself go and then started to pull at the dress. Get her naked and wank over her. Like they did in the films. They liked that. There was no way into this dress. He turned her onto her side. There had to be a way into the dress.

Then he stopped.

He'd rolled her over. Off the pillow. Onto her side.

"You leaked on my bed," he screamed.

Wes turned in horror, and looked at the back of the woman's head. Missing. Completely. Not even rudimentarily patched up. The hole just hidden under a fucking wig. And her brain. It had turned to slush. All the rocking back and forth. Her brain juices had leaked.

She'd wrecked the pillow.

Wes jumped out from between her legs. Off the bed. "No," he whined. "Now you're getting it on the sheets." He sighed. Looked down at himself. Flaccid. Nothing turns a man off like decomposed brain leakage.

"Fuck."

He pulled his clothes back on and hurried along the landing to the airing cupboard. Pulled an old blanket out the bottom. Back to the bedroom. Spread it out on the floor. He ran around to the other side of the bed and shoved her as hard as he could to roll her off the bed.

Too hard.

She rolled all right. Brain sploop coming out of her like her head was a salad spinner. Wes could do nothing, but watch in horror. It created a line of pinkish grey matter across the bed. Up him. A little made the ceiling. There was even some on the wardrobe on the other side of the room. He hurried back to the blanket. She'd rolled off it. It was on the carpet too.

"Cunt," he screamed at the top of his voice. He raised his foot up, losing his temper, and jabbed it down as hard as he could on her gut. She made this sound like a rhinoceros shitting, and the room filled with some noxious gas. Hidden deep within her for months.

Months.

Wes put his hand over his mouth. "Nope." He ran from the room and slammed the door. "Right." He stormed downstairs to the door to the cellar and yanked it open. Went down there too. Cold down there. It was always cold down there. He went to the shelving on the left hand side of the room and counted the spaces. There were three left. He was planning on keeping her upstairs for a while. But she was moving in, down there, *now*. With the rest of them. His eyes rolled down the other shelves. Eight filled. Shelves built to take the weight of a body. The cellar air conditioned down to about three degrees Celsius. Twenty four seven. It was like a harem of poon. All his previous victories. Better than notches on bedposts. Why not keep the bodies?

If she didn't stink so much, he might not have put her down there. After all she wasn't quite a victory. But he had managed to get inside her. All the way. So she probably still counted.

Anyway. He went upstairs and pulled a dirty tea towel out the washing machine. Wrapped it around his head and tied it off, like a face mask.

Back to the bedroom.

He could still smell her through it. But it would do. For now.

He rolled her back on the blanket and dragged her out onto the landing. Down the stairs, careful not to spill anymore … brain.

He was going to have to shampoo the bedroom carpet now. Which was trouble. And because he hadn't even gotten what he wanted. It wasn't worth that trouble.

Down into the basement.

Heft her up on a shelf. One of the bottom ones. So she didn't leak on the others. Wes stood there staring at her. This wasn't ideal. Too long and they were decomposed. Not long enough and they smelt. Somewhere in the middle and they were leaky.

He tapped the side of his head.

Maybe he should try making his own?

CHAPTER 5

Why hadn't he thought of it before? It was simple. Just go out and find the right woman. And ... well, you know. Had to be the easiest way. And ... *and* it avoided all that fucking digging. There were probably downsides. But he couldn't see any of them.

Now he was standing in the supermarket.

Staring at women.

He had noticed that security were aware of him, but he'd moved from the fresh fruit to the fridges. Put a couple of lemons in the trolley. That seemed to pacify them. He was currently hunched over, had a microwave meal in his hand. Watching this lovely looking young lady. She was shopping for a family by the look of it. Put him off. If he'd wanted kids, he'd have kids.

But she *was* pretty.

There was someone else just behind her that he'd been watching since the fruit and veg. Had a basket. Not a trolley. Seemed to be weighing up a selection of meals for one. Promising. She took a couple of vegetarian ones.

Wes looked at his. Liver and bacon in gravy with mash. Well. No one was perfect. It really didn't matter if she was a veggie. Oh. She's off.

Wes dropped the ready meal into his trolley absently and continued around the store. Following her. She went along one aisle into the dairy products. Started packing in those drinks. Good bacteria ones. Whatever they were. He hoped they didn't give you a loose bowel.

Not after the mess last time.

Then she popped fake milk in her basket. Must be a veggie. All that fibre. That bacteria thing. It was surprise she could get around the supermarket without needing a shit. Off again. Wes followed her down the next aisle. Then the next. Most of the way around the shop. He was dropping occasional items into his basket. Didn't want any of them. Just watching her. Becoming slowly convinced that she was *the one*.

He slid along, close to her. Got a good look. Like window shopping. He was so close he could smell her. She stank of flowers and fruit. That, he was not used to. Sure the graveyards tended to smell like that. But not the girls.

Never mind. Smells can be washed off.

She glanced at him.

Fuck.

He was looking. Staring. Like a weirdo. She gave him a half smile. It looked … uncomfortable. Questioning why he was staring at her. Fuck it. Do something. Say something. *Cover yourself.*

"Do you know where the …" he stopped. Where the *what* was? Now she was focussing in on him. She'd heard. This couldn't have been going wronger. Say something. *She's looking at you like you're freak now.* "… ready meals are?" There. Said something.

Cool off. Relax.

She looked in the trolley. His trolley. At his ready meals.

Well, *shit*.

Wes looked down, following her stare. Then said, "Oh, well. Yes." He looked back at her. She was flushed red. Like he'd said something embarrassing. Well, he had. But that was beside the point. "What?" he asked.

"It's just …" She touched her face. It was sweet. "I don't know." She turned away. Thoroughly embarrassed. "It's just that, when you asked the dopey question, and you were all embarrassed, I thought you might be trying to ask me out."

Wes looked at the floor.

Well. This was just perfect.

Part 2

~

DOLLY

CHAPTER 7

Dolly scrabbled through the dirt. Fucking hell. It wasn't supposed to be like this. The fucking psycho just turned on her. About an hour ago, she and … what was his name again? … they were sitting on the park bench. Middle of the evening. All touches and romance. Little teasing kisses. Then he changed. Tried to take it too far. He got all grabby. He'd torn her dress. She was sure of that.

But now she was laying in the dirt. Hiding in the dark. The park wasn't that big. And they had chosen it because it wasn't well lit. He was going to find her soon enough. She looked around. Couldn't see jack or shit. There had to be something around there she could use as a weapon. Felt like she was rolling about in the dark. All she could see were shadows. Tree cover was too heavy for much in the way of moon light. She got to her knees. Squinted into the trees. Bushes. There was a light a little way off. The single light that all shit parks had, just so you could find your way to the centre after some rapist had jumped you.

She stood. Spun in a circle. She could see other lights in the distance. Like edge of the park distance. But she couldn't fathom the best way to get there. Two choices—the way she saw it. Run at the fences shouting *rape*, or crawl at them silently. She never was one for subtlety.

But before she could start running and/or screaming, he grabbed her from behind. He slapped one hand on her shoulder and spun her to face him. In the dark he didn't look quite as handsome as he was when they met. He had some sort of rugged coolness to him then. Now he looked … dirty, she supposed.

Then the cunt punched her in the face.

She stumbled backwards, out of his grip, but didn't lose her footing. He stepped in, towards her. She assumed he was going to rape her, then kill her. As was the usual arrangement of these things. She put her hand up to her face. Felt the warmth of the blood on it. She glanced down and saw that her bra was exposed. He *had* torn her dress getting all handsy with her, and she really liked that dress. It came for a real shop. Not the internet where most of her things came from. Bastard.

He came at her. Forward. Hands out.

Dolly didn't know what to do. She didn't have any self-defence training—although in hindsight, that should have been on the agenda for years. Well, too late now.

Striding in.

Blind moment of panic.

Dolly kicked out. The one thing she could see herself doing. She stepped in towards him, as he was her, and she punted for all she was worth. Didn't know if it was going to do anything. She'd seen in the movies and on TV, but those things exaggerated everything. She also didn't know if it was going to contact.

But it did.

Toe punt of excellence, right in the crown jewels.

He froze up. Looked like he'd shit himself. Fucking good. Both of his hands ploughed down between his legs and he staggered a little forward. Dolly toppled subtly as she stumbled back, not used to hefting great kicks into men's balls. Not that she would have classed this fuck as a man. Not after what he did.

He was still standing there when she'd finished getting her balance back, teetering like he was going to fall. Dolly stepped forward, punched him on the side of the head. She didn't know if she'd balled up her fist wrong, or if she was just shit at it, but it hurt like a bastard. Must have hurt him too, because he fell to the side. Grunted out something. Seemed to try to say something too, but she wasn't listening. She kicked off her shoes. High heels. She'd worn them for him. *For him*. Arsefaced piece of … she stepped forward. Even though it was a pleasant night, the cool damp of the grass seeped into her stockings. She stamped on his head.

Made her feel better.

CHAPTER 8

He grunted again. Tried to burble out an apology by the sounds of it, but she wasn't going to let him. He'd gone too far. It was far too late. She looked around. She wanted something to hurt him with. Something she could inflict the same level of fear, embarrassment, anger, on him with. Something that she could say, *I did that* about. Her eyes fell on her shoes. On the grass. Cradled by the dark. She picked up one of them. Walked to him. He was still cradling his pathetic bollocks. Had some blood running down his face, too. From where she'd kicked him. A slight pang of sympathy misted over her, but she shook it off. It *was* only a slight pang. She dropped to her knees. "Why?" she hissed. "Why did you do that?"

He looked at her. He really did look sorry. But it wasn't good enough. "I didn't mean to. I just … just …"

Just what? Where's the excuse?

"… you're so good looking …"

True.

"… and I couldn't help myself."

And there it was. No meant no. It did in Dolly's book, regardless of what it said in his. She raised up the stilettoed shoe, and smacked him in the face with it. Spikey bit first. At least, that was her intention. She did it with force though. She knew she must look pretty pathetic. On her knees in the middle of the park. Middle of the night. Slapping some pathetic arse around with a shoe. So she made up for it by hitting him hard. As hard as she could.

He wailed out. His hands went from his balls to his face. She rocked back slightly. Tried to get a better look. When he moved his hand to the side she could see that she'd drawn a gash down the side of his face. Missed his eye socket by an inch. Went from the hairline, by the eye, the ear, and down to the back of the jaw. As first it didn't seem to bleed. Surprised her. It looked deep. Nasty. Then it finally came. Like it was waiting for permission or some shit.

He rolled over. Tried to get out the way of her. On the grass. Balled up like a fucking baby. Maybe even crying. It was hard to tell with all the other bawling. She waddled on her knees after him. By the time he'd stopped rolling, and righted himself enough to look to see where she was, she was over him again. "Fucker," she said.

The shoe went up again. Back. Down hard. *Hard.* She clipped him full with the heel. The spike. It was made of metal. The shoes were some cheap knock-off of an Italian brand, but they were surprisingly good. Hard wearing. Cheap. Win-win, really. But this time the spike sunk into his temple. It made a sickening noise when it did. A sort of hollow thud.

Then he started to spaz-out. Having a fit or something. He was … vibrating … for lack of a better word. His eyes open. Staring into the darkness. His arms had dropped down to his side and he was convulsing. Weird gurgling sounds coming from his throat. Like he was drowning. Suffocating.

Dolly stared at him. She'd done that to him. She looked at her shoe. It was still impaled into him. White foamy gloop was frothing around his lips. He was dying, she thought. She'd broken his brain. And he was dying.

She realised her fingers were shaking slightly. Excitement. She'd never seen anyone dying before. She worked in a travel agents. And now this guy was dying because she'd hit him.

And it made her warm. Tingly. She was enjoying it, more than she felt she should be.

What the fuck?

She knelt there. Watching as his convulsions slowed. Like he was coming out of it, but he didn't seem to be … what were the words … *getting better*. He looked up into the canopy of trees. Vaguely.

Dolly reached forward and touched the shoe. Sticking out of him. She felt a burning sensation between her legs when she did. She gripped the shoe and the sensation turned up. She was focussing on her own breathing now. Not paying any attention to his. Or if he was. She was breathing hard. Like she'd been making out with this guy for hours.

To be honest, she'd never been that interested in sex with the men she saw. Maybe that was why she was still single. But she'd never really *felt* it. She just played the part, they'd get bored of her, there'd be tears. They'd split up.

She was looking at his guy. One hand on the

shoe. She realised the other was cupping her breast. She could feel her nipple hard under her bra. "Oh my God," she said. "This isn't right." It wasn't. There had to be something wrong with her. Dolly slipped her fingers inside her bra and pinched herself.

Electric shocks of pleasure dug into her like the nails of a lover writhing beneath her. "Oh, God," she muttered. Gave a worried glance to his face. He wasn't looking at her. He was just staring. She wondered if he was dead. Part of her didn't care. She knelt up and pulled her dress over her thighs. Put her hand between her legs. Stroked herself. Over her panties. She could feel the wetness there. With no effort. She hadn't had to think about anyone or do anything. She was just wet. This never happened. She made some half-hearted apology. Didn't think it really mattered now, as she thought he was probably dead. She slung one leg over him. Straddled him. Her hand firmly placed on her cunt. She was reaming it up and down. Slipping and sliding the fabric against her skin.

Moved her fingers into her panties. Felt the raging heat on her skin. Slid her fingers inside herself. She realised she was still holding the shoe. She let it go. Pulled the part of her dress that was still covering her chest off, and down. Flipped her bra straps off and pulled that down. The cool air flicking at her naked breasts. Her fingers deep inside her. Exploring a place she'd never been before.

Sure, she'd masturbated. But only in the most vanilla way. And only in the bath. No clean up.

And there she was now. Finger fucking herself in the park in the middle of the night. One hand pinching her nipples, her tits, the flesh. Anything to cause the sensations that rode her body, as she started to hump the body beneath her.

Then he moved.

The fucker wasn't dead.

She looked down at his face. His eyes met hers. Wide. He was confused—rather understandably—but also in pain.

And he had a shoe sticking out of his head.

He made the noise of an eighty-year-old man waking up to find his day nurse with her hand in his wallet.

"Fuck," Dolly screamed. She was so close to bursting, and this sudden movement had jarred her position. She did all she could think to do. She grabbed the shoe and twisted it.

He screamed out. Bucked. It brought her back. Close. She was going to cum. He was moving his hands now. Fuck it. He was trying to get her off.

And not in that way. Cunt.

She yanked the shoe from his temple and grey-brown liquid jettisoned from his head like he was under pressure in there. He was still moving. Might have been brain fluid. If it was, would anyone notice? She smiled internally at her wit, and then raised the shoe like a dagger.

Stabbed it down as hard as she could into his

face. Aimed for the heel to go into his eyes. First time she missed. The metal slid down his cheek gashing to his eye, catching his bottom eyelid. Enough to stop him from trying to remove her while he raised his hands to protect his face.

She brought it up again quickly. Down on the other eye. The unprotected one. Straight in. The metal heel slipping through the soft wet tissue of the eyeball, a white mush of eyeball filling splooting up, like cum from a younger man. Onto his face. Stopped moving.

She still had her fingers up her snatch. She hadn't stopped pounding herself. Even when he was trying to stop her. She fought to climax. Screaming as she reached it. Her hand, free of the shoe, pushing against his face, trying to hold herself upright as the orgasm ripped through her. She pulled her hand from her panties, pulled air into her lungs.

Leant back.

Her tits pointing skyward. Her hands back, holding her cowgirl over his corpse as blood let freely from his destroyed eye, mixing with the white pus from within it. She giggled.

What a ride. Pulled herself off him. Onto the grass. She glanced down to him. "Bet you weren't expecting that?" she said. "Me either." She pulled her shoe from his face and wiped the heel down his jeans. Put it back on. Got the other one on. She dressed herself as best she could. Bra back on. Half a dress. He'd torn the strap on the other side. No problem.

Dolly looked in a circle. She'd run around wildly before they fought. The bench. The one he'd started it on. Her bag was still there. She saw it. Went and sat. Her legs were shaking. She was breathing deeply, trying to bring herself back to the real world. She needed to process what just happened. Opened her handbag and pulled out a safety pin, fixing her dress well enough to be able to get back home with no questions asked.

She started out the park.

Her mind was racing.

She'd never wanted this before. Not like this. Wild. Animal. It made her feel alive. Fucking hell. She smiled to herself.

This needed investigation.

CHAPTER 9

So fucking frustrating. This wasn't working. She'd done all the research, and found all that the internet could offer. And all the recommendations—all of them—pointed her to a film called Nekromantik. And it just wasn't working for her.

She was sitting in the dark, in her flat, on the sofa, the TV on. The film playing. She had wine. Even brought herself a bunch of roses for that romantic feeling. But she wasn't. Feeling it, that was. She had scoured the forums online to find out what film people recommended she watch because she found the concept of death … erotic. And this was the film they had come up with. Ugh. It was some low budget shitty horror film with loads of titties in it.

But fine. She'd sat through it, hoping that the themes and visuals of this woman, horny for some corpse bone, would do what the other night had done. She'd sat through the whole thing. Waiting.

Nothing. It was sorely disappointing.

And somewhat confusing. The film wasn't exactly what she was expecting, but close enough, and it didn't really get her anywhere. Not being a connoisseur of horror in any way, shape, or form, hadn't helped. If she had been, then maybe she'd have known this was what got her going years ago.

She sipped her wine.

All those wasted years. When all she needed to

do was ... well, what? She waved at the TV. Whatever the fuck this was, wasn't it. She picked up the remote and flicked the DVD back to the menu. Opened the trailers menu. Played that.

These seemed more generic in terms of horror. Some spooky house shit. Something about a cabin in the woods. Clowns.

Boring.

Fuck it. She turned the DVD off completely. Back to the TV. Flipped it to the BBC. She looked at the time. Nearly time for the news. Fine. She should keep an eye on that, anyway. They'd found the body in the park. Some poor dog walker the next morning. That was three days ago. His name was Jason Couzins. She'd remembered it as soon as they said it. It had eluded her until that point. The police had said that he was brutally murdered. Beaten to death. That was hardly true, but she supposed they wouldn't want to give too much of it away, not with what *really* happened. She wondered if they had found evidence of some of the other things that happened. DNA or whatnot. She probably left plenty of it behind. That would probably fuck them up. She smiled.

Yes.

She imagined a scene from Midsommer Murders or something like that. The one with the bloke from Bergerac in. Standing over the body in the morgue. Some serious looking old man with a white coat on, jabbing at the body, while Bergerac looked serious. "Cum on him," he would say. "Female ejaculate over his chest."

"So they had intercourse beforehand?"

"No," he replied. "It was post-mortem."

"Interesting." Taps his teeth with a biro or something.

Interesting indeed, she thought. Oh. Here was the news. She missed when they used to start the news with the Big Ben chimes. Anyway. Red screen. And … voice.

New leads? They said *new leads* in the murder case in the park. Hm. Shit. Well, it can't be too much. She certainly hasn't had a troupe of bobbies trying to bang the door down in the last few hours. And besides, they wouldn't be able to match her DNA or anything. She'd never so much as had a parking ticket.

Of course, she had considered turning herself in, but, well, she didn't want them to think she was weird or anything.

They started showing footage from *the scene*. The park. It looked so different in the day. She smiled. That was where it happened. That tree. She could tell because of the placement of the park bench.

She rested her hand down on the mound just above her slit. She was only wearing her panties. Nothing else. She was expecting the film to do the job. Waste of time getting undressed, really. She rolled her fingers back and forth. Watching the footage of the park. The newscaster, a solemn sounding older gentleman. He kept using words like bloody, brutal, murder. Acts of violence.

She realised she was fingering herself. Subconsciously.

Fucking hell. That was it.

It wasn't bollocks like horror movies. It was the realness of it. The tangible-ness, if that was even a word. The … actuality.

That was what got her off. What got her hot.

Actual violence. Not pretend violence.

Dolly looked down at herself. She was breathing harder now. Fingers slipping through her wetness.

Well, that's a bit of problem, now. Isn't it?

Fuck.

CHAPTER 10

Okay, okay, she was telling herself over and over. *There has to be other ways of doing this*. Or not doing it. What was to say that she needed to do this sort of thing again? Celibate. She could just give up on it.

No.

There was an evil little voice inside that hadn't been there before. It was—she believed—the personification of her horny-ness. Having gone far too far through her life putting up with inconsistent and, frankly, shitty romantic trysts that rarely got her off, *or even began to get her on*, she now wanted to fuck. She wanted to feel like that. It was the one thing, right now, in her life, that she was one hundred percent sure of.

She was sitting in the pub looking at a man on the other side of the bar.

She just wasn't sure *how* to do it. The bloke over the other side. He looked like he would be all right. She paused. Thought about what she was considering. Did it matter what he was like? Not really. Not to her. Not at all, actually. She was going to cut him up.

And just the thought of it made her want him.

She'd been watching him for about half an hour. He was alone. He might have been waiting for something. For someone. But she didn't think so. Hadn't kept looking around like he was. That would have been the biggest give away. And he didn't seem to be in there on the pull, either. Didn't seem to have any interest in other people. Certainly hadn't seen her watching him. She glanced down at herself. She was dressed pretty well. Had on a dress with a plunging neck line. Sort of thing she thought a man would like. Spent some time on the internet looking at what men wanted.

She didn't *want* him to have what he wanted. Fuck no. But she needed to lure him. So she had given the appearance that she was sexually available—hence the dress. Apparently men were absolutely hopeless at spotting hints. Also, she was in a quandary about the amount of makeup to wear. Generally, the opinion among the men she spoke to, was that she shouldn't wear too much.

Well, fuck them. But she tried a little *less is more*—as was suggested. Again, it was only to lure the man. Not for his pleasure. She really didn't want to make this any harder on herself than she actually had to.

Drew in a breath. Christ. She was actually going to have to make the first move, wasn't she? Maybe she should have gone somewhere more meat-markety. Taken whatever came her way in one of those clubs where everyone is just there to get laid.

She pushed herself off the stall and went around the bar, taking her vodka tonic with her. That was the other thing. She *needed to be drunk enough to be approachable, but not too drunk to be sloppy*.

Men were insufferable arseholes.

Got to the bloke. Didn't notice her. Fine. As expected. She slipped her drink onto the bar. "Is this seat taken?" she asked. Seemed reasonable.

The guy looked around the bar. There were, probably twenty seats along the edge of the bar, and this place was empty. Fucking desolate. He was clearly making a point about her having plenty of choice and *why the hell did she want to sit there*? Utterly clueless. She smiled at him. Tilted her head so she looked a bit like a confused dog. Men liked dogs, right?

He shook his head finally. "No." He turned back to his drink.

Dolly got up on the stall. He was ignoring her. Clearly. He even seemed to have turned a little further away from her than he was sitting previously, just so he didn't have to interact with her. The barman walked around from the other side. Gave her a look. He could tell what she was doing, and this doofus was missing the point completely. He came over to the two of them, paused. "Can I get you two anything?"

"Oh," Doofy said. "We're not together."

"Shame," he said. "You make a lovely couple."

Doofy looked at Dolly for the first time. It was like he needed someone to break the ice for him. Thank God. He smiled. Had a nice smile. "Can I buy you a drink?"

Well. It was about time.

CHAPTER 11

Dolly pulled him by the hand down the street. Doofy's name, as it turned out, was Stewart. He seemed nice enough. She was taking him back to her place. She was weaving about a bit, pretending to be drunker than she really was. Not sloppy, of course—perish the thought—but just drunk enough to take a complete stranger home with her. Doof—Stewart was two sheets to the wind. Didn't matter to her.

He was an insurance something, something, in town for some reason. She'd switched off. He was down on business and having a pint whiling the evening away. That was good enough for her. No one was waiting for him anywhere and the Travel Inn sure as shit wasn't going to mind if he never came back for the night.

She wasn't well practised at this *art of seduction* stuff, not when it came to pulling men in bars and taking them home. But it was surprisingly easy. All those Hallmark films dictating the chase. Bullshit. Promise him a warm coffee, a hot body, and a blowjob. An hour and a half of movie saved. He had fallen for it hook, line, and sinker. She'd promised him nothing and expected nothing in return. He'd be back on the road in a couple of days and they'd always have Birchingate.

At least, she would.

He just *thought* he would.

What he was going to get was something else. Probably less to his taste.

They got to the flat. Dolly turned at the communal entrance and put her finger over her lips. "Shh." She made a lot of noise shushing him. "The neighbours," she said, knowingly.

He nodded, equally knowingly.

In all truth, the old town house was three storey's tall, converted into three flats. The girl in the basement wasn't there. She seemed to have done a bunk a week or more ago. And the old woman in the ground floor flat was away visiting family. She knew, because the old bird had asked her to water her plants. Left her the key and everything.

So the building was completely empty.

And she could do what she wanted to this guy. With this guy. *With this guy.* She stabbed the key at the lock a couple of times before sliding it home. "Bodes well," she said to him. He let out a light giggle. She didn't think he was drunk either. Not really. Just playing on it. You know, because he was being a fucking sleaze taking some random girl home and fucking her, before disappearing into the wide world of insurance.

Not that it mattered.

She opened the door and the two of them entered the hallway. She made creeping, silly gestures as they passed the old woman's front door. To hers. In.

There was a set of stairs right inside the front door. Up to the landing. It wasn't a particularly big flat. One bedroom. Living room. Box room that was supposed to be a second bedroom. Bullshit. A Kitchen, and a fairly good-sized bathroom. Dolly turned and threw her arms around Stewart's neck, leaning in to kiss. Had to be careful, because the two of them nearly lost their balance and went flying back down the stairs. Wouldn't do any good if they both ended up dead there, now, would it?

She smiled as she pulled away from him. "Coffee, first?"

"First," he snorted as he laughed. "Aren't you presumptuous?"

"You *don't* want this?" She gestured down her body, flowing. From tit to toe.

"I do," he said. Low. Growly.

She growled back. Felt a little silly, but ho-hum. Play the game. "So," she said. "Coffee?" She really had little idea what she was doing.

"Oh," he responded. "Okay."

CHAPTER 12

The two of them sat in relative discomfort in the kitchen as they made small talk, drinking shit instant coffee. Perhaps the offer was stupid. She thought that was what you did. Maybe he was stupid too. He was the one that said yes. And she'd forgotten how shit her coffee was. And drinking coffee at this time, she was going to be up all night.

Although that was the point, wasn't it?

She was so laboured by the trauma that was spending time with *Stewart*, as the two of them sobered up, that she considered pulling the bread knife from the kitchen block and plunging it into his neck. Not what she had planned at all—although similar in many aspects—just to *end* this bullshit.

The thought of doing it, however, sparked that feeling again. The one in her loins. She remembered why he was there, and decided she really should get on with it. Dolly put her coffee down. "What the fuck are we doing drinking shit coffee?" she asked.

Stewart looked surprised. Actually, Stewart looked like he was trying to think of a reason to go home. "I … I don't know," he stammered.

"Blowie?" she asked.

"Well." Stewart put his coffee down next to hers. Stood. "Don't mind if I do."

Dolly could feel the wet, stickiness of her slit as

she all but dragged poor Stewart through to the bedroom. He didn't seem to mind.

She had his hand, pulled him in, and left him standing by the door, while she swept across the bedroom. It was all set up to do as she planned. The bed was made. She'd put a plastic incontinence sheet under the regular sheets, because she was sure there was going to be mess. She'd also made sure to dispose of the packaging for it carefully, because she guessed for most men, having a women who pissed herself in the middle of the night would be a turn off. Only most, mind. Men were, largely, pigs. Anyway. Under the mattress was the chef's knife from the kitchen block.

And attached to the headboard, carefully hanging behind the bed, were cuffs. She'd made them herself from cable ties. Just like the internet had suggested. She'd found herself at some interesting places researching all this, that she didn't want to think about now, but had written down the addresses, so she could investigate further. Later.

She turned, unzipping her dress at the same time, letting it fall to the floor. Left her wearing her undergarments and high heels. The internet had told her that men were *dogs*—possibly not in a bad way, it was hard to tell—and they tended to like slutty women. Dolly didn't know anything about that, so further research on more reputable sites had told her, lacy bra and panties. Stockings were a must. High heels in the bed. Sealed the deal.

Stewart was grinning.

Already pulling his belt open. His suit jacket dropped to the floor behind him. Fucking hell. This chap didn't hang around. She glanced down at herself. Well. Neither did she, from his point of view, so fair game.

Trousers open. Had on blue boxers underneath. Nothing grand. Kicked his shoes off. Christ. What did have a dental appointment to get to? Socks stayed on. Classy. Shirt open.

He was on the bed, scooting over to the middle of it.

Well. Men *were* dogs. She grinned as if this flourish of activity impressed her. Granted she did need him on the bed. But she wasn't concerned with any of the rest of it. She'd planned what she was going to do. To the letter. It was simple. She was going to tie him to the bed—cable tie him to the bed—naked, and then cut off his cock. It was going to be hard, so should be fairly easy.

Actually, that was as far as she had gotten. She was noting all this down in the notepad she had in the bedside drawer last night. After she'd bought all the items she needed. Including the knife block. She wouldn't want to carve a chicken with the knife. Not after … that. Anyway. As she had gotten to that part, playing it out in her head, she'd been overcome with need, and buttered her own muffin. A term she leant on a website called Fortune, or something like that. She did like the term, though. Buttering the muffin. She smiled to herself.

Realised Stewart had his cock out. Rock hard.

Expecting a blowjob.

Oh, shit. She was just standing there, reminiscing.

She got on the bed next to him. Handled his cock a little. Stroked it. Didn't really want to put it in her mouth. He was making all these happy noises. Good. "I've got an idea," she said. She turned and straddled him. Took his hand up to the headboard and reached behind, getting the cable tie cuff. She slipped it on him. The internet said that he would not object to this part. No man did.

He watched her. She could feel his cock throbbing hard while she did. Internet was right. Good. She did the same to the other hand. Stewart seemed to be *right up for it*. "You're a dirty girl," he said.

Didn't know the half of it.

She was getting more excited now. She could feel the tingling inside her. Tingling that wanted to be released. Dolly pulled her bra off. Much to Stewart's pleasure. He made some lewd comment that she didn't even hear. There was another voice in her head. She was listening to that one. It was telling what to do next.

How to sate her desire.

How to get off. Get off now. She stuck her hand down the front of her panties and started to finger herself. Felt so good. Having him helpless. About to die. Blood was going to go everywhere.

"Don't forget about me," he sneered.

How fucking dare he? "As if I could," she said. Dolly leant to the side and slipped her hand down, between the mattress and the bed. Carefully. She didn't want to cut herself, did she? She pulled the knife out. Waved it in front of him.

His face changed. Dropped. He looked confused for a second. Then it turned to horror. Absolute fucking horror. He started babbling. Something about this all being a silly mistake and how if she'd just let him off the bed, then he'd be on his way, and that was all right wasn't it, he didn't mean to be such an arsehole, and he did have to get up for an early meeting, and my was that—

CHAPTER 13

Dolly lost her shit at him and slashed the knife across his bare chest. It was a brand new knife—never cut so much as a sandwich with it—but it *was* from an infamous budget supermarket that tended to sell shite.

The blade cut his skin. Certainly enough to shut him up. But there was no blood. At first. At first, she thought it had just bounced along the flesh, and he'd only stopped talking because of shock. Then the blood came. The slit cut from below his left nipple, across his whole chest and over the right. He looked down at himself. A blunt look. One that said, *how am I going to explain this to my wife?* Before he screamed, and the blood seeped out. Only slightly worse than a papercut, at least, it looked that way. Dolly looked at the knife and nodded her appreciation.

Stewart was ranting.

Although his erection hadn't gone away.

So Dolly pushed her panties to the side and slipped on to him. May as well take advantage while there was advantage to be had. She started to bounce on his cock as he protested, too much, she felt, as she could still feel him hard inside her. Throbbing. He clearly approved of something she was doing. She pressed her hand into his chest. Into the blood. He let out a weird otherworldly noise as she did. Hurt, she expected. But she held the knife to his face. "Fuck me," she said.

The rise of her urges were fast. Quickening, the harder she rode him. The more fear he had in his eyes as she waved the knife dangerously close to his face. She could feel him softening inside her. The blood pumping somewhere else. "You stay hard, or I will cut you."

He whimpered. Cock going flaccid. *Flaccinating*, she thought. A little smile. Then she slipped off his useless junk. Fucker. She stabbed the knife into his side. Above the hip. In hard. Twisted. She slid her hand, crimson with his juices, into her panties. Started to frig herself. If that was only way she was getting it, she could do it perfectly well herself.

He squirmed under her. Bucking like a fucking bronco. She pulled the knife out. His blood jettisoned out. Onto her legs. His body. He started screaming for help. Pathetic cuck. Stabbed the knife in again. Same place, different angle. In, more across the body. He stopped screaming. Blood trickling from his mouth, and she twisted it again. She could feel his sticky blood mixing with her vaginal leakage, swirling together as she pleasured herself. Ready to cum. She wanted to explode. Already knew she wanted it more than once.

She pulled the knife out. His intestines (maybe) pulled out with the knife. A tube of something, sticky and squishy, undulating as something was passing inside of it. Blood lurched over his flesh, running down into the gap between them. Where her hand was inside her underwear. Her fingers deep in her cavern finding the right spots. Making her back arch.

He was looking pale. Staring at her. He was still alive. She was sure of that. He was in shock, she thought. That's why he wasn't moving. Or screaming. Suddenly she rocked back hard, yelling out to a deity that hopefully had his eyes averted. Then his son. The orgasm blistered through her like nothing she'd ever felt before.

But she couldn't stop. She arched back towards him. Blood over the two of them. Grinning like a mad woman, she pulled the knife up, over her head. Fingering herself harder. Faster. She plunged the blade into his chest. Deep. To the handle. It sank in with far greater ease than she expected. He choked. Coughing blood forward. Out onto his chest where the knife sat. She let go. Leaving it there for him to stare at, and used one hand to hold her panties back, the other pleasuring deeper. Deeper.

Finding another orgasm.

Pulling it free.

Dolly screamed. She screamed like she had been the one stabbed in the chest with a ten inch knife. Choking on blood. Bleeding out.

She slowed.

Rocking herself back and forth on his corpse. She looked down at herself. His blood, still warm, basting her naked flesh. She pulled her fingers from herself. Gently fingering her clit. Keeping the warmth there. Rising it up, lowering it down, as she watched his blood flow ever slower from his body. Out. Onto the sheets.

She reached forward with her free hand and took the knife. Pulled it from his chest. Blood squirted like cum from the wound. Out. Spraying onto her. Wetting her more. She made a yawning noise as another orgasm rose in her. "Fucking hell," she blurted. "Oh." She came fast. Hard. Loudly.

No neighbours.

Bouncing her body in time with her finger flicking herself slowly, faster. Fastest. Slower. Pleasure rippling through her until she could take no more. Slowing. Stopping. Looking at Stewart as she realised her sweat was mixing with his blood, turning her a cute hue of pink, flooding onto the sheets. Her juices joining it all. The two of them there on the bed, amidst a cocktail of fluids. His. Hers. She giggled. "Oh yes," she said. "That's the stuff." She rolled off him. Next to him on the bed. He was growing more pale. The blood was drooling out of him now. Gravity, not pumping, doing the work.

She lay on the sheets. In the primordial soup of human goo. Ran the tip of the blade over her belly, absently. "Oh," she said. "That's sharp." She looked at the clock on the bedside table. "Christ, it's getting late." She had work in the morning. Dolly got up and looked at the body. The mess. "Huh." She pulled the sheets from under the edge of the mattress, the plastic one too, and hurled it over him. She would deal with him later. Looked down at herself. She could feel her heart beating hard inside her. What a rush. She checked the base of her feet like she'd been painting the ceiling and wanted to make sure she wasn't going to tramp anything anywhere, and headed for the shower. She pulled a chunk of Stewart from her as she passed the wastepaper bin, and dropped it in. Didn't want to block up the bath, now, did she?

CHAPTER 14

Dolly was sitting in the office at about two in the afternoon when she decided what to do with Stewart. After her shower last night, she'd thought *fuck it*, and slept on the sofa. Left him in the master to languish. She would clean him up after work the following day.

She'd been sitting there for at least an hour now, staring off into space, trying to decide what to do with him for the best. Chop him up. It was the best thing she could come up with. Bin liners? Put him in bin liners, yes. Chop him into little pieces and put him in bin liners, and put him out with the bins.

Bin men in the area were pretty fucking hopeless anyway, so dropping a few bits of Stewart in the bin—at the bottom—shouldn't be a problem. They'd never know it was hers. Not after it was in the dustcart. Problem solved.

She frowned. Glanced at Debbie on the other side of the office. She was clicking her pen. Damned infuriating sound. Whatever. Wait. She couldn't put *all* of Stewart in the bin in one go. That was silly. She'd have to put a little of him in every week. Well. Once a fortnight, because that was when they took the black bins. Couldn't put him in the recycling, could she? Not a very responsible thing to do. Contaminating all the cardboard. So, a little a fortnight. She sat back. Thinking. Probably going to take, what, two months to get rid. Shit. She was probably going to want to go again before then. She could still feel the ambient warmth from her orgasm now. It was like it was in her blood. Had a taste for it. No. Couldn't wait another two months. She'd need to get rid of him quicker than that.

A trip to the local tip? Hm. Harder to get away with, she suspected. Loading him into the car like that. Then unloading him at the other end. What if one of the bags broke? Bits of Stewart spilling out in front of a hundred other people all pushing to dispose of their hedge trimmings.

Something … else.

She could buy one of those grinding, shredder, things for garden waste. A mulcher. Mulch him.

No. Silly. She lived in a flat. Where would she store a mulcher?

Cut him up into little pieces, put him in the bin liners. Then … load him in the car. Take him out in the middle of the night, and dump him in public bins. The ones on the side of the road. She'd have to be careful, bit suspicious stopping and chucking waste into public bins. But it would work. They emptied them out a few times a week. Probably before he'd start to smell, but even if he did. As long as no one *saw* her dumping him.

Scott free.

Perfect. She'd pick up bin liners on the way home. She'd need a saw of some sort too. A hack saw? Was that right? She could probably get one in the supermarket. Get the bin liners. She was short of a few other things too. Could do the groceries, while she was there. Been meaning to start a new diet. Something more fruit and veg based. Less toxins.

Dolly pulled up to park in the supermarket. It wasn't her usual. She thought it smarter to use one she wasn't used to being seen in. Especially when she planned to buy the body disposal stuff. Not that she was worried about getting caught. She was infallible. Probably. It was a good plan, that's all she was saying.

Whatever.

Went to the front of the store. Picked up a basket. She shouldn't need a trolley. Not for what she wanted. Damn it. Not used to the shop. Picked up a couple of lemons. Actually. Fuck making this stuff. She decided to go and get a couple a ready meals first. In the centre of the shop she stopped and looked down the aisles at the signs above them. DIY was labelled right at the other end. Fuck it. *Get the hacksaw last*, she thought. They'd better sell one. Even if it was shit. Prove a point, wouldn't it? She glanced at the security guard. He was ignoring her. Watching some weirdo standing there with a trolley staring into space. Pah. Who does that? She shook her head, and headed to the ready meals. Jammed a couple of them into her basket. Labelled vegetarian. To be honest, she didn't really care what they were. She probably should have just gone and got the disposal stuff and caught up with her shopping another time.

Around to the next aisle. Grabbed some probiotic stuff. Pulled some almond milk from the fridge and stuffed it down next to the meals.

She looked up.

That weirdo. He was there. In the aisle with her. Staring at her. Approaching. Slowly. What the fuck did he want? Oh, my. She'd read about this sort of thing. Men trying to meet women in supermarkets.

He walked up to her. "Do you know where the ready meals are?" he asked.

Dolly looked at him, then down into his trolley. There were already ready meals in there. He was looking for an excuse to talk to her.

Huh.

That's kinda sweet.

CHAPTER 15

Jesus fucking Christ. She didn't think it was going to happen *that* quickly. She was arched over the bath. Stewart was in there. Naked. She was sawing at the bone just below the elbow. She'd tried hacking his arm off through the elbow, but the bones and the joint and whatnot made it near on impossible.

Hacking.

Fucking cheap arse, supermarket fucking hacksaw. Probably couldn't have cut through balsa wood with it. A brisket. *Fucking butter*. And now she was getting frustrated.

After meeting with Wes in the supermarket, the two of them had gotten talking. He seemed nice. If not a little strange. But that was okay. And he'd actually fumbled his words around to eventually asking her out.

Tomorrow.

Which was fine. No. Better. Great. He was going to be her second. It was fantastic. She got wet just thinking about him. The deed. The blood. But she wanted something different next time. Didn't want to repeat what she'd done with Stewart. That felt a little like she was cheating on him. But anyway. That was like … twenty-four hours away. Shit. She looked at the arm. Half hacked off. Then at the time. Fucking hell. This was going to take forever. She made a mental note not to try and do this two nights running again. Not with work in the middle, anyway.

She started sawing back and forth again. She was covered in blood. She knew it was going to be messy, but not like this. No. She put her pinny on, thinking that would be enough to catch the occasional sprays of blood. Wouldn't be much would there? Most of it had leaked out onto the bed. And the rest of it, well, it would have solidified in his bum or something. Right? She should have paid more attention in school—not that they teach you this in Home Ecc—because apparently, at least in the following day, the blood in the human body is still quite, quite, runny.

So the pinny had gone for a burton, and now she was naked. It seemed best. Less mess. She had the roll of bin liners on the floor next to her, and, so far, had only used one. A hand. The one from the arm she was now trying to detach.

Far slower than she expected to.

She was going to have to call in sick to work tomorrow anyway, but at this rate, by the time she was due to meet Wes, she'd only have loped off the one arm.

Fucking hell. This was hard work.

She took a breather. Christ. Leaning against the bath she looked at the shit hacksaw. Needed a better one. A much better one. Maybe better than anything she could buy locally. Something off the internet. Some website that specialises in cutting down trees. Manly site. She should order it under a pseudonym. Something like Vaughn Jakobson. Sounded Swedish.

Manly. Bearderly.

Yes.

She tossed the shit saw to the side and got up. Went to the kitchen. That knife block. The one she got the knife from. That she was never going to use to cut meat.

Time to cut some meat with it. She'd boned a chicken. How hard could it be to do the same with a person? Shit. She looked at the carpet. Bloody footprints. God damn it. She shook her head, and grabbed the cleaver from the block. Then thought better of it and took the whole chopping block.

―――

Three in the morning. She'd packed Stewart into the car and was away. Cleaned up. Even the flat. The bed. Everything. Apart from the seven bags of human body parts in the boot, there was no evidence whatsoever that Stewart had happened. She was never doing this again. Not on this timetable.

So silly.

She looked in the mirror. *Drive normal*, she told herself. Not that it mattered. Does anyone ever see a police car after two? After the clubs have turned out. There was no one on the road, that was for sure.

She pulled up in the middle of the high street. Got out. She looked around casually. Went to the boot. Pulled out a bin liner. Went to the bin on the side of the road. Had at least a days worth of shit in it. Good.

Dropped the bag in. Not a fucking clue which body part it was. Didn't care.

Back in the car.

Onto the next bin.

Part 3
~
WES & DOLLY

CHAPTER 16

Wes was sitting in the pub. They'd agreed to meet at seven. It was a work night. That was fine. He could take her back to his place. She'd be fine with that. She seemed cool. Crack her over the head. Then he could put her away for the evening. It was Friday tomorrow. He could save her for Friday night. One day in the basement would be fine, wouldn't it? He scrunched up his face, and looked at his phone. Ten past seven. She was late. Maybe she wasn't coming. Fuck it. Maybe she'd made him. Worked out he wanted her for more than her mind. More than her body.

He looked at the barman. He was standing there, polishing a glass. *Why do they do that*, he thought. Back in the day, sure, but now. It had just come out the dishwasher. And it was a Thursday. It wasn't like he was super busy. Maybe it was just something to do?

So fascinated was he in the barman's glass polishing, he hadn't noticed Dolly coming in. She looked around. Waited by the door. Waved. Got his attention.

Wes pushed himself from the chair and smiled at her. She looked tired. Like she'd been working too hard. Maybe she needed a day off.

Well, she probably wasn't going into work tomorrow. He smiled to himself as she approached.

"What's so funny?" she asked.

"Oh, oh, nothing." Wes wiped the grin from his face. She looked fucking nice. He was going to enjoy it. She was going to be fresh. Cool. Fragrant. A new experience. Maybe he could keep her for a few days? Use her more than once? He had no idea how long she was going to keep in the basement. Within his experience, they were usually pretty much fucked before they got there. Before he got to fuck them. He stifled another smile. Didn't want to have to explain *that* joke. Jeepers.

Dolly greeted him and sat down at the table.

"Drink?" Wes asked.

"I'll have … a Bloody Mary."

Wes nodded, went to the bar and ordered it from the glass polisher. And another pint for himself. He was on Guinness, for some reason. He watched her, waiting for the drinks. She was sitting looking out the window. She was sweet. So sweet. And pretty. He hoped to be able to complete his plan without … damaging her in any way.

He was quite excited, to be honest. Looking forward to the chase, as it were. See if he could get her back to his place. All in the pretence of romance. Didn't matter too much if he couldn't though. Pretty sure a quick bosh over the head and she'd be pliable enough for him to bundle into his car.

Shit. What if she had *her* car? She wouldn't want a lift home. The bartender put the drinks down in front of him and Wes rolled a ten over to him. He waited for his change, looking at the pint. Hm. Probably shouldn't drink too much either. Shouldn't get plastered before taking her home. Then he looked at hers. Well, if she was drinking, maybe she'd gotten a bus down or something.

He picked up his change from the bar where the bartender had put it, in a dribble of someone else's spillage—nice—and then took the two drinks to Dolly. When he put hers down, she said, "Thank you so much. I'll have to move on to coke after this, though. My car's around the corner."

Fuck.

Wes smiled, like it was nothing. Because it *was* nothing. He could deal with it. He picked up his glass. Laughed. "Maybe you can give me a lift, then," he said. He was only joking, but she grinned at him.

"Well, of course," she said. "Drink up. I might like to take advantage."

———

Wes had taken her at her word. Or perhaps she was an expert at whatever it was that was going on. Wes wasn't sure anymore. And he kept referring to himself as Wes in his head for some reason. He looked at the beer. It wasn't Guinness. Too brown. She'd gotten the wrong drink. He told her he'd get the next round, but she'd insisted.

Christ, how much had he had?

He blinked, trying to get the room to stop

swimming.

Fuck it. Look out the window. He could see the harbour in the distance. Focus on that. Try to get it level.

"You okay?" she asked, sitting back down. She tossed him a packet of pickled onion flavour crisps. She had cheese and onion. Why did he ask for these? He liked ready salted. But Wes opened them and started to stuff them in his mouth.

He tried counting the glasses on the table. Six. Were they all his? Or were some hers? She'd moved on to diet pop after the first drink. Could be hers. Hold on. There were seven glasses now. Shit. He hoped she still wouldn't mind giving him a lift home. Tonight—the tonight *he'd* planned—was off. Get her to drop him at home. Had a lovely evening, thank you. I'd love to see you again. Friday night? Of course I'm free.

He ran the conversation in his head.

"Drink up," she said. "It's nearly closing time."

Fucking hell. He was going to have to call in sick tomorrow. If he could get his eyes open enough to do so.

CHAPTER 17

Dolly let the car idle at the traffic lights for some time. She patiently waited for them to turn green. Glanced to Wes. He was staring out the window. He certainly had put it away through the evening. He was awake. Or at least, his eyes were open, but he seemed … vague. She rested her hand on his knee, and he looked at her. Smiled. Looked a bit … dribbly.

Didn't matter. She was all about what was on the inside. That was what counted. Not the outside. Not of the flesh. It was the inside. The warm sticky inside.

She blushed and turned back to the lights. Changing.

Pulled away.

She glanced over to him, then back to the road. He was looking out the window again. Turned left. Towards her flat. She'd told him she'd take him home. He seemed happy about it, but hadn't even thought to tell her where he lived.

Oh well. She grinned internally.

Drove under a street light that went out as they did, and then popped back on as they drove on. Wes made a strange cooing noise. Pissed as a newt. Dolly pulled up on the side of the road.

"We're here," she said, sliding her seatbelt off.

Wes looked up at the house. "Cool." He continued to stare like he was buffering. "Where's here?"

"My place." She opened the door. "Come on." She'd never tried this before. Had no idea if this sort of shit worked. To be honest, she hadn't expected it to be *that* hard to get some geezer who hit on her in the supermarket—*the supermarket*—to come back to her place to fuck. Actually, all said and done, what with the research she'd done online, she had been led to believe that all men were pussy-hungry dogs what would be on her like a jackal. Marie-Claire was going to get a strongly worded email over the weekend about their disgracefully misleading slurs on men. And how disappointed she was.

Getting him drunk.

Wes looked at her and smiled. She wasn't sure if he even understood. He just patted her on the leg and got out. Winding his way towards the house. Dolly quickly got out and locked the car, hurrying over to him before he fell.

He looked like he was going to fall.

"I was supposed to take you back to my place," he said.

Yes, yes. "Were you?" Dolly replied, the smallest hint of sarcasm in her voice. He wasn't going to understand. She slipped her arm through his and led him to the front door. Still had her keys in her hand from the car, and opened up. She held him to her as they went in her front door, traversing the stairs to the first floor, and to the landing.

She took him into the living room and plopped

him down on the sofa. Regretted it immediately. She should have just taken him to the bedroom. She'd already set up the bed like last time because it seemed to work so well. Now he was lushing about on the sofa. Probably couldn't get him up if he passed out.

Dolly smiled at him. Slipped her shoes off and kicked them in front of the TV. "Coffee?" she asked.

"Sure," he mumbled in response.

Dolly went to the kitchen. Flicked the kettle on. What the fuck was she doing? She should have just dropped him off at his place. It would have been so much easier to agree to meet up with him again in a couple of days. Then she wouldn't have to worry about any of this. She could just bring him back here sober. Get him in the sack. Tie him up. Have her way. Bob's your uncle, Fanny's your aunt. She pulled a mug down for him. She didn't even fancy one. Put a couple of sugars in it. Thought again, and popped another two in. Sugar rush. Get him up. An extra heaped spoon of coffee too. She poured the coffee in the mug and took it through to him. Sober him up a bit.

There was still fun to be had.

CHAPTER 18

Wes took the coffee and sipped it. In all fairness, the spinning room had subsided to a slight wobble and a feeling of abject sickness. He mumbled some sort of failed thank you to the woman. What was her name? Oh, yes. Dolly. He looked at her. A little … sheepish. Another sip of the coffee. She was standing there in the doorway. Expectant. Fucking hell. She wanted to fuck, didn't she?

The haze was starting to clear a little. Maybe it was the coffee. Maybe it was the sitting down. *Maybe it was because he'd stopped drinking whatever the fuck it was that he was drinking.* Christ. What a cocktail.

He glanced at her. "I'll be with you in a second," he said. Shit. That sounded unbelievably cuntish. "Sorry," he mumbled. Sort yourself out or she's going to throw you out. Maybe he should leave? Just go. Find a taxi to take you home. Find your car later. Wherever it was now. Down the harbour somewhere.

Or.

Or.

Wes looked over to the woman.

He could do it there.

Wes smiled at her over the lip of the cup. "I really am sorry," he said. Slurring slightly. Fighting to control it. "It's the drink. I must say," he slipped the coffee down in front of the sofa. "You are gorgeous." He was no good at this. Why was he bothering? He could just go over there, and throttle her. Right now. Squeeze the life out of her. Force the air from her lungs. Force her heart to take its last.

Then fuck her.

On the sofa.

The bed.

The kitchen floor.

The options were endless. Well, not endless. The flat was pretty small. Then he could leave. Pretend he was never there. If they tracked him down after finding her corpse, well, *no*, he could say, *she dropped me off at mine. I never saw her again. She said something about going to a club. Looking for some action. I was so out of it.* Yes. That was it.

I was so out of it.

He started to stand and the beer got the better of him. He sat back down. Room span a little before easing. He was going to have bide his time. Wait until he was in the right place. The right frame of mind. "Why don't you come over here," he said. Put his hand out, waving her forward. "Let me get to know you."

Wow. Just wow. If this works ... fuck me. She's coming over.

Dolly slipped across the room. She looked great. Sexy. Horny. Slightly disappointed, but he was working on remedying that. She sat next to him.

Hopefully she didn't kick the coffee over. Wouldn't want to stain the rug. Actually, it wasn't going to matter in a little while. Christ, she was waiting.

Make a move, fool.

Wes leaned forward and kissed her. Shit. Her lips had a tinge of coolness on them, from being outside. Hadn't had any coffee, like him. Made his lips feel hotter than hers. Wes closed his eyes and kept kissing her. It wasn't what he wanted, but it wasn't repulsive, either.

She responded.

That was good, he supposed. There was something about her. Something different. Something he couldn't quite put his fingers on. She oozed a ... gothic-ness ... no, that wasn't the right word ... macabre-ness about her. Some sort of darkness, in the way she looked at him. Some sort of *death*.

Whatever it was, for the first time in his life, Wes was digging it. Shit. He was getting hard. In his jeans. He really didn't expect that. Put his hand up, resting it on her breast. Over her shirt. Dress. He'd forgotten. Whatever. He used his other hand to rearrange his junk. It was jabbing in the wrong direction. She touched him. Her cold, warmth. He knew that didn't make any sense, but fuck. He ...

He ...

... wanted her.

His tongue was in her mouth. It was hot in there. Not something he was used to, but something he could certainly work with. Hand up, under her clothes. Seeking out flesh. Found it. Again, warmer than he was used to, but there was something that was pushing him forward. "Oh, my, God," he muttered, trying not to drool on her at the same time. He wanted to take it to the bedroom.

Did ... did he still want to kill her?

He wasn't sure. He could. Guarantee the outcome. But if she wanted to fuck him, and he was going to enjoy it, why not keep her around? She'd stay fresh longer. He felt his erection waver. Not the time to be thinking about that. Should be thinking good thoughts.

Dead nuns.

Always got him off.

CHAPTER 19

Wes was touching her all over. It wasn't repulsive, Dolly thought, after all she'd played this tune many times in the past. This time, however, she was just using it. Had her own end game of sorts. He seemed awfully keen. Had his tongue in her mouth and everything.

Better lure him into the bedroom.

She grabbed the first thing she could think of that would do that. Wrapped her fingers around his cock. It was sticking up, hard in his jeans. Not a bad size, given that it was being held tight by his clothing. Huh. Might find some use for that before there was no blood left in him to get it hard.

He responded to the grab, gasping and pulling away from her.

Dolly stood, releasing him. "Come on," she said, nodding her head towards the door. "Now you're feeling better." He stood. Obedient little puppy. She took his hand and led him to the bedroom.

First things first.

Get him restrained. Once that was done, anything was possible.

She pulled him into the room, led him to the bed and turned him to face her, back to the bed. He wobbled a little. Still a little blood in his alcohol stream, it appeared. She smiled and dropped to her knees. Undid his belt. Pulled it open. Opened his jeans. She was kind of excited to see the contents, to be honest. She opened the zip and his cock swung forth. His pants still holding him in place. They weren't exactly attractive. Maybe he wasn't expecting to get this far? Whatever. They were staying on. She looked up at him, smiling, but he seemed to be focussing more on standing still and not swaying back and forth. Fine. She pulled his jeans to his ankles, then his pants. She looked at his cock. It was definitely the biggest she'd even seen this close. She'd seen a little porn recently—only in the aims of research, of course—and some of those were bigger, but they say the camera adds ten pounds. She grabbed the shaft and gave it a little wank.

He let out a moan. Good. Keep him *on side*, as it were. She thought about undoing his trainers, but thought better of it and just yanked them off. Then she could pull his jeans off.

This was all fucking exhausting, but she was sure it was easier this way that once he was on the bed.

She then stood. Noticed he was looking at her. Probably expecting a blow job. Well, he wasn't getting one. She wasn't into that. She pushed him back onto the bed. That was easy. He had the wind resistance of a dried leave. He flopped down. Let out a little giggle. Then he straightened himself.

Excellent.

He was up. Head on the middle pillow. Good. She leant over, and took his arm. Again. No resistance. She restrained it. He made some noises, and suggested she was a dirty fucker.

He didn't know the half of it.

She went around the bed. Did the other arm.

That was that, done. Right. She stood and looked at him. Leaned over his body and touched his cock. It flexed as she did. Still grew in girth. Wasn't expecting more, but fine. She was wondering if it was going to be comfortable. Maybe if she drained some of the blood from him, it might get a little smaller?

Maybe? Who knew?

She rounded the bed again. Pulled her blouse open and dropped it to the floor. A good distance from the bed. Didn't want to get it messed up after all. She slipped her skirt off. Noted that he was writhing about, clearly enjoying the view.

She could take her time now.

CHAPTER 20

Wes writhed on the bed. Fucking hell. What had she done? He thought it was going to be some bullshit tied-to-the-bed-with-a-pair-of-garters shit or something. She was dropping clothing on the floor. He looked up at the binds. Fucking cable ties. What the fuck was her game? How was he supposed to do this now? He wanted to fuck her, sure. But the killing was still definitely a possibility. It really all depended on whether he could finish or not.

You know, if she was still breathing.

Still, he looked down himself. At least she didn't say anything about the scabby shorts he was wearing. He didn't really expect her to see them. Not living her, anyway. He could feel his cock straining. This was weird. Unexpected. She was pulling her knickers off now. Facing the other way so he could see her arse. Looked good. Better if it was cold. But much like the rest of her, it was probably burning hot.

He was so fucking conflicted.

He still wanted the burning hot arse. Wes yanked on the cable ties again. Nothing. These things were not coming off.

She disappeared from the room while he was looking at his own dick. Shit. What now? He hoped he hadn't pissed her off, whilst looking at himself, not her.

She came back in. Good. She had a pair of

scissors. Fucking kitchen ones. The ones that can go through anything. What the fuck was she going to do with those? *Say something.* "What are you going to do with those?" Better.

She straddled him on the bed. Just below his cock. Left it to bounce between them. Jesus Christ. She leant forward.

Started to cut his t-shirt off.

Fucking hell. "I need that to get home," he said quietly. Which was true. What kind of woman does that? She could have pulled it from him before she tied him down. One of his favourites too. Shaun of the Dead. Had Nick Frost on it. She dropped the scissors on the bedside table, started to run her hands over his skin. It was nice. He liked it. She could have been colder. Couldn't seem to shake that feeling, in all fairness.

But never mind. She seemed to be keeping everything up. Which was a first.

She pulled her bra off. Her tits were round. Not large, but heavy. Something he wasn't used to. Most of his dates had lost all their perks in that area. He reached his head forward. Tried to reach them with his mouth, but she pulled back. Touching them herself.

Frustration was growing.

Not just sexual frustration. He was getting pissed that he was no longer in any control. Something he had always had. *Look*, he told himself, *at least you don't have to spend hours digging a fucking hole.*

Now she was fingering herself.

She seemed to be having fun. Wes looked down himself. *She* seemed to be having fun. He didn't even seem to figure into it. Wes found himself wondering what he was going to have for tea tomorrow night. She leant forwards towards him. He was starting to lose interest now. Wished she was dead. And he could get on with it. Whatever he was feeling in the living room was numbing. She slipped back, again. Away from him. Had a … fucking great knife in her hand. Stay calm. Last time she did something like that, she just fucked up your t-shirt. *Just*. Fucking hell. She wrapped her fingers around his cock. Made sure he was properly hard.

Which he wasn't until she did that. Something about the knife. Perceived threat. Made him gloriously erect. In fact. Hold on. He was pretty close to … oh. Blimey. She slipped her body forward, and down onto his cock. She was wet. Must have been dripping. Couldn't see, but she felt like it. That was pleasant. Something he'd not felt before. Her heat, wrapped around him. Made him want to blow. This burning sensation, started in his gut. Worked its way down. Felt a bit like diarrhoea. With all he'd drunk it could be. Shit. Literally.

Maybe he was about to cum?

She pounded hard on him. Squealing. She seemed to be really enjoying it. Then the knife went up. Wes screamed as he came. The fear. That was what did it. Fear. Heat. Unexplained attraction.

She stuck the blade into him. So hard. So

violently, at first he didn't feel it. Then wet, blistering pain. It started to drown him. He could feel it in his lungs. Stopping the breath from getting in there. He coughed. Choked something up. He could hear her. She still sounded like she was having a grand time. Maybe she hadn't realised what she'd done. Maybe that was it. She was going to open her eyes and see that she'd actually cut him and stop.

Call an ambulance.

No. She'd pulled the knife out now. She was off his cock too. Finger fucking herself. And finger fucking the giant chest wound he had.

Fucking blood everywhere.

CHAPTER 21

Oh. My God. The orgasm rippled through her, over, and again. One. Twice. She had her fingers deep in the cavity that the knife had opened up in his chest. Her other fingers deep within her. Found the spot. That spot. Didn't even know it existed, but it worked like a fucking light switch. On. Off. On. Off. Over and over.

She pulled her fingers from Wes's body. He'd spewed blood up her arm all the way to the elbow. She caressed her breast. Smearing him over her flesh.

Then there was a smell. The fuck was that? It was coming from him. She looked at him. He had a strange little smile on his face. Frozen there. His eyes were loosely hung open. His cock was still hard. Not hard-hard. but hard enough to fuck if she still wanted to. Which was the last thing she expected, now he was dead.

But what the fuck was that smell?

It smelt like shit.

Oh, God. She scooted backwards as quickly as she could. Fuuuck. He'd shit himself. And all that Guinness. It was like baby shit. Fucking wretched stank, fucking runny, shit.

Shit.

She heaved. Dry heave. No. It was coming.

Dolly vomited right there. Covering the shit,

blood, and naked flesh. It drooled from her mouth. Out. Dinner was in there. Looked like cat food now. Used to be cottage pie. Never eating that again.

Then the smell of that hit her.

She was going to do it again.

Dolly rolled from the bed like a ninja. Onto the carpet. Remembered to check the soles of her feet. Clean. Out to the bathroom. Flee the stench.

She hit the shower hard. Had the fuckers shit up in between her legs. All up in her slit. Guy must have fired it out like a paintball gun. As the water ran, she started to laugh. There was a funny side. The water was pooling around her feet. Shit and bits of Wes clogging the plug hole.

She poked at it with her toe.

Right. She needed to get rid of the body. People would ask questions, of course. She put her head under the shower. *No*, she would say. *He was hammered. Absolutely out of it. Made a drunken pass at me, so I just dropped him off. He didn't even tell me where he lived, so I left him at the side of the road. He disappeared completely? Suspected foul play. Wow. Dodged a bullet there.* Yes. That was it.

Dodged a bullet.

Her thoughts dropped back to his cock. Wondered how long it would stay hard for.

You know.

Post mortem.

About the Author

Ash is a British horror author. He resides in the south, in the Garden of England. He writes horror that is sometimes fantastical, sometimes grounded, but always deeply graphic, and black with humour.

Printed in Great Britain
by Amazon